No Pickles for Annabelle

PRAISE FOR *STORYSHARES*

"One of the brightest innovators and game-changers in the education industry."
– Forbes

"Your success in applying research-validated practices to promote literacy serves as a valuable model for other organizations seeking to create evidence-based literacy programs."

- Library of Congress

"We need powerful social and educational innovation, and Storyshares is breaking new ground. The organization addresses critical problems facing our students and teachers. I am excited about the strategies it brings to the collective work of making sure every student has an equal chance in life."
– Teach For America

"Around the world, this is one of the up-and-coming trailblazers changing the landscape of literacy and education."
- International Literacy Association

"It's the perfect idea. There's really nothing like this. I mean wow, this will be a wonderful experience for young people."   - Andrea Davis Pinkney, Executive Director, Scholastic

"Reading for meaning opens opportunities for a lifetime of learning. Providing emerging readers with engaging texts that are designed to offer both challenges and support for each individual will improve their lives for years to come. Storyshares is a wonderful start."
- David Rose, Co-founder of CAST & UDL

No Pickles for Annabelle

Dollie Stiemsma

STORYSHARES

Story Share, Inc.
New York. Boston. Philadelphia

Storyshares
Story Share, Inc.
24 N. Bryn Mawr Avenue #340
Bryn Mawr, PA 19010-3304
www.storyshares.org

Inspiring reading with a new kind of book.

Interest Level: Middle School
Grade Level Equivalent: 4.8

9781642611717

Book design by Storyshares

Printed in the United States of America

Storyshares Presents

1

Annabelle was seated motionless on the school's swing. Her green eyes peered out from behind the safety of her sunglasses. She quietly watched as the popular kids in her class sat under the leaves of the old maple tree to discuss summer plans. She didn't have to strain to hear their giggles and lively chatter; she also didn't have to guess the topic.

Hamilton School's seventh grade girls spent today's recess talking about summer camps, family trips, and sleepovers. Annabelle sat alone. Biting her quivering lip to fight back tears, she thought about her own summer break. She knew her days wouldn't consist of playing on hot sunny beaches or talking late into the night at sleepovers.

Annabelle was the daughter of a pickle farmer. Her family tree included three generations of cucumber farmers that grew and sold baby cucumbers to the local pickle company. Annabelle knew summer break meant working all day in the sun-baked fields of her family's pickle farm. She would help to harvest the tiny two-inch cucumbers that the farmers called "pickles."

Annabelle knew that pickles of this size would develop rapidly and need to be picked every other day. Shifting her eyes down to her soft hands, she remembered how those small cucumbers had sharp points that would prick her small, delicate fingers, leaving them calloused and ugly.

When school started, her hands looked like her father's. It took the entire school year, but her hands finally began to look like they belonged to her. Pink nail polish topped her nails again.

There would be no camps or trips to talk about with her classmates. There would just be millions of little prickly pickles to pick all summer long.

I must be the only kid on earth who dreads summer, she thought.

Secretly, she didn't know which she disliked more: school or pickle farming. They were both difficult for her. She couldn't wait to finish school, but she also dreaded the start of pickle season.

Oh well, there's nothing I can do to change my summer, Annabelle thought. *This is my life.*

With her attention focused on the giggling under the tree, Annabelle hadn't even noticed how the afternoon breeze was now encouraging her swing to move back and forth.

Annabelle grabbed the metal chains holding her swing and leaned back. She pointed her rainbow-colored tennis shoes towards the sky. Her wavy blonde hair almost touched the hardened dirt. She closed her eyes and let her imagination take her away from thoughts of prickly pickles. *I'll think about being an acrobat.* She smiled and let herself swing almost upside down as her fantasy of flying took her to a happier place.

Annabelle's favorite pastime was swinging upside down. She had attempted to swing from just about any place—swing sets, monkey bars, and even tree branches. Once, when she went with her family to the local library, she tried to hang upside down on the library's handrail.

She couldn't explain why she loved to swing upside down . . . she just knew she was happiest when she was doing it.

Anabelle had been swinging contentedly for a few moments when a sudden thought snapped her back to reality. Her eyes sprang open, her legs flew to the ground, and a look of terror came over her face. The SPELLING TEST was after recess! She had almost completely forgotten about it.

Spelling was Annabelle's least favorite subject. No matter how hard she tried, she couldn't seem to sound out words correctly. She had studied very hard last night. She had practiced over and over as she did before every spelling test, but she knew in her gut it wouldn't matter. She would still get a big, red "F".

"It feels like the only world I can spell is *failed.* I've sure seen it enough," she groaned.

As if taking the test wasn't torture enough, Annabelle's teacher, Miss Dunkin, always asked the students to pass their test to the person sitting on their right for grading. Annabelle had the unfortunate luck to have the smartest boy in her class, Jack, seated to her right. Not only was he the smartest boy, he also had the biggest mouth. He always told everyone Annabelle's score. She knew that today wouldn't be any different.

2

As the recess bell echoed throughout the playground, Annabelle felt the impending doom of another failure. There was no escape. She headed back to class at a snail's pace.

I spent extra time last night studying, so maybe this test won't be so bad.

With a glimmer of hope and a sigh, Annabelle sat down at her desk. She put away her sunglasses and pulled out a piece of paper and pencil. She tried to appear confident as she prepared herself for the dreaded exam.

"Ok, class," said Miss Dunkin. "I hope everyone had fun during recess because it's time for our weekly spelling test."

The class grumbled as Miss Dunkin picked up the list of words. "I know everyone studied hard, so please take out your paper and pencil."

Miss Dunkin faced her class and read off the first spelling word. Annabelle knew her doom was no longer just impending . . . it was here. "Your first word is *disappeared*. As in, the jump rope has *disappeared* from our classroom."

Annabelle struggled to spell the word. She wished *she* could disappear. She tried hard to sound it out: D-I-S-P-E-R. It didn't look right, but she wrote it down anyway.

Miss Dunkin walked through the aisles of desks as she gave the next word. "Imagine," she said. "I can't *imagine* life without trees."

Annabelle struggled to spell the word: E-M-A-G-I-N. Again, she felt it was wrong, but she didn't know how to go about correcting it.

Imagine a life without another spelling test, Annabelle thought. There was no point wishing for a world without spelling tests.

Annabelle struggled through the entire test. When the test was over, Miss Dunkin asked everyone to pass his or her test to the right. As Annabelle handed her test to Jack, she hoped maybe this time it would be different.

Her hopes were instantly smashed when Jack flashed his evil smile. He picked up his red marker and said, "Miss Dunkin, is *disappeared* ever spelled D-I-S-P-E-R?" The entire class began to snicker and giggle. Annabelle hunched down. She wished she could fade into the floor.

"Now, Jack," said Miss Dunkin, "how many times have I asked you not to call out in class? I'll give you the correct spelling of each word. You are to mark wrong answers. You don't need to add any comments."

Jack smiled smugly and made a check mark in the air with his red marker.

Miss Dunkin said, "Let's begin."

The rest of the afternoon didn't go any better for Annabelle. As she struggled with her social studies assignment, Annabelle couldn't help but notice how her classmates seemed to breeze through their work. They even had time for a lively discussion about who finished first.

Annabelle returned her attention to her badly scribbled answers. She flipped her pencil over and began erasing another misspelled answer.

As she blew away eraser pieces, she muttered a sound of hopeless defeat. She started to try again, but the dismissal bell interrupted her.

A slight smile appeared on Annabelle's mouth. Oh, how she loved the sound of that wonderful bell. Finally, after feeling like a total failure, this horrible day had ended. Annabelle scrambled to finish her last question and clean up her desk. She snatched up her pink and purple backpack and ran for the door. Her timid smile broadened, almost reaching her green eyes. Only a few more steps and she would be free.

3

"Annabelle, can you wait a minute, please?"

When Annabelle heard those words, she knew what was coming. Her teacher wanted to talk about her spelling test. The smile vanished as quickly as it had come.

"Yes, Miss Dunkin," was all Annabelle could say. She slowly turned away from freedom and back to the dreaded classroom.

Miss Dunkin was smiling, standing between her heavy oak desk and the chalk-stained blackboard. She held out Annabelle's latest spelling test. "I know you can do better than this with your spelling," she said. "I don't understand why your scores haven't improved like everyone else's. I've decided to give you another list of words to study this weekend. On Monday, I'll test you during recess. I just know that with a little more work on your part, you can improve."

Miss Dunkin smiled as she handed Annabelle a new list of words. "See you Monday, Annabelle. Make sure you study those new spelling words this weekend." Miss Dunkin was still smiling as she turned and walked out into the hall.

Stunned, Annabelle stood in the empty classroom staring at the list of new spelling words. She could hear the buses leaving the school parking lot—she'd have to walk home. An overwhelming hopelessness filled her while tears of shame ran down her cheeks. She quickly wiped them away. She lost no time in escaping the school and hurrying toward freedom.

4

Annabelle ran until she reached the family's long, dusty driveway. She willed herself to slow down and breathe. She readjusted her favorite backpack and dragged her shoes in the gravel as she walked.

She had made it through another week of school, but she still couldn't believe that Miss Dunkin had given her another list of spelling words! Didn't her teacher know that she still wouldn't get any better? Another wave of despair washed over her as she dragged herself towards the house.

Annabelle's little sister was waiting impatiently on the farmhouse's back steps. Emily looked like a country girl in her red cowgirl boots. Yellow ribbons hung from her pigtails.

"Where have you been?" demanded Emily, tapping her boots on the doorstep. "What took you so long? Did you forget we promised to help Daddy right after school? Because you're so late, I had to do all the work myself."

Annabelle dropped her backpack on the doorstep. "What's your problem, Emily? You love every minute of working in that big old barn with Dad. Plus," she said shortly, "it's none of your business why it took me so long."

Annabelle didn't want to tell anyone about her conversation with Miss Dunkin - especially not her smarty pants little sister who wouldn't understand.

"I have homework, an extra credit project, and don't forget my hour of piano lessons," said Emily. "You know full well I have very little free time." The constant tapping of Emily's foot made her pigtails sway.

"Oh, go away," said Annabelle.

Emily grabbed the doorknob. "I really don't understand why you have to be so nasty," she said. Without waiting for Annabelle to explain anymore, Emily stomped inside.

Annabelle was left standing alone on the back steps. She instantly regretted being mean. Emily hadn't done anything wrong. It wasn't Emily's problem her big sister had to stay after school.

Everything had always come easily for Emily. Annabelle believed her little sister would never experience humiliation. She would never have to stay after school to talk about spelling test scores.

Annabelle recalled all the late nights seated at the kitchen table hopelessly staring at blank pieces of paper. Emily would enter the room, solve the problem, and give a winning smile as she strolled away.

Why? How could two sisters be so different? she wondered. Annabelle released a quiet sigh, unable to answer those questions.

5

    Annabelle went inside. She could hear her sister running through the house yelling, "She's finally here!" She also heard voices coming from the living room. She knew that the voices were her mom and dad, but whose was the other voice? Curious, Annabelle tossed her backpack onto the kitchen counter and hurried into the living room.

    Annabelle was ecstatic to find her favorite aunt sitting on the comfortable old sofa engaged in a conversation with her parents. She loved Aunt Sylvia. Nearly all of her favorite memories were of spending time with her. There were the times Aunt Sylvia took her shopping, stayed up late to watch movies, and ate junk food. There were also the girly makeovers they would give each other. Annabelle felt the wonderful memories replace the painful memory of her school day. She hurried over to hug her favorite aunt. The day had just gotten a whole lot brighter.

"Annabelle, you were late coming home from school today!" scolded her mother. "Did you forget it was your turn to set the table? I need you to set it now, it's time for dinner."

She turned toward her mother to beg for a few minutes with her aunt but thought better of it when she saw her mother's lecturing eyes. It was a look that said, "You had better get into the kitchen immediately and finish the job!"

"Yes, Mom," Annabelle answered reluctantly.

As Annabelle set the table with the good silverware, she began to ponder her family's life as pickle farmers. *Why has the entire family always worked on the pickle farm except for Aunt Sylvia? Did Aunt Sylvia ever have to spend her entire summer with those prickly pickles*

Annabelle realized she didn't know what her aunt did during the summer months. She had always wanted to know the answer, but she had never thought it was her place to ask. *Maybe tonight I'll just ask.*

Annabelle did her usual inspection of the table as she laid down the last fork. Pleased with her work, Annabelle hollered, "Table is done! Let's eat!"

6

The mashed potatoes, broccoli, and spinach salad had all been gobbled up. Only a few pieces of Mom's famous mouthwatering fried chicken were left. Annabelle knew if she waited much longer, she would miss her opportunity to ask her question. She spotted Emily chomping on a pickle. This gave her an idea. Annabelle smiled warmly at her aunt and passed her the bowl of pickles.

"Thank you, Annabelle," said her aunt. She took the bowl and passed it on without taking a pickle.

"Aunt Sylvia, why don't you have to work on the pickle farm like everyone else in our family?" Annabelle asked. "Don't you like pickles?"

Everyone stopped eating and stared at Annabelle. She couldn't believe she had just said, "Don't you like pickles?" She hadn't planned on sounding so impolite, but it had just come out. She was desperate to know the answer! *Was she the only person in her entire family that hated pickles?*

Annabelle felt a kick from Emily's boot under the table. "Ouch! Why did you do that?" Annabelle moaned. "I was just curious. You didn't have to kick me."

"Then don't ask ridiculous questions, Annabelle. Everyone enjoys picking pickles, don't they, Daddy?" Emily said, wrinkling her nose and glaring at her big sister. Emily was always kissing up to Dad.

Setting down his fork, Dad smiled proudly at Emily. He reached over and tugged on her pigtails. "That's right, everyone loves pickles. So, please pass me one before you eat them all," Dad said.

"It's okay, Emily," Aunt Sylvia said. "Annabelle can ask me any question she likes."

Emily turned to face Annabelle, popping the last bite of pickle into her mouth. She rolled her eyes, but didn't say another word.

"To answer your question, Annabelle," said Aunt Sylvia, "I would have to say that I don't dislike picking pickles. I was just never very good at it. I was always pulling on the pickles too hard and bringing up the entire vine with the pickles. I wasn't very good at finding the smaller pickles hiding under the leaves either. I would end up leaving many of the smaller pickles behind.

"Everyone always said I was the worst pickle farmer they had ever seen," she laughed. "I finally discovered that my talents were not for farming. It's your father and uncles who have the real talent for being great pickle farmers."

Annabelle stared intently at her aunt. *What did she mean about having a talent?* She had never heard anyone talk about having a talent for pickle farming before.

Aunt Sylvia smiled warmly at Annabelle. "Your mother is talented in math, which she uses for her bookkeeping. She's also a great manager; she runs this home and farm while caring for you and Emily. But I believe her greatest talent is cooking these delicious meals! The truth is, everyone has talents," she explained. "Most people have many different types of talents. The important thing is to identify and develop them. Did you know I have a talent for being creative but not for cooking? My mashed potatoes taste like cardboard."

"Taste like cardboard!" Emily laughed, putting her hand on her mouth to stop pickle spit.

"What are you good at, or what do you enjoy doing Annabelle?" asked Aunt Sylvia.

Annabelle just sat there across from her aunt, looking confused.

"I know what some of my talents are!" Emily proudly offered. "I'm good at reading, writing, drawing, math, and, of course, my piano. But you can't forget," she said excitedly, "I'm the world's best pickle picker."

"Yes, you are," Dad smiled proudly. "You are our overachiever, and your mother is the world's best cook and best mother."

"That's right," agreed Emily. "I'm the best picker and Mommy's the best mommy!"

"That's very nice of you to say, Emily. Now will you please clean up your plate?" Mom replied.

"I don't know," Annabelle said timidly as she glanced down at her plate. "I don't have anything that I'm good at. I just know pickles are prickly and gross, and I hate spelling."

"Annabelle, honey, we know you don't enjoy picking pickles, but remember, if it weren't for the pickles, you wouldn't have nice clothes or decent meals," said Mom.

"I understand what Annabelle is trying to say," Aunt Sylvia replied as she reached over and squeezed Annabelle's hand. "She just doesn't feel she's cut out to be a pickle farmer." Aunt Sylvia looked tenderly at Annabelle and asked, "Now what is this about not liking spelling?"

Annabelle dropped her head and stared at her food, trying to look interested in the fried chicken on her plate. The embarrassment of the question showed on her face. Through the lump in her throat, Annabelle mumbled, "I'm just not any good at it."

"I wasn't very good at spelling either," Aunt Sylvia replied.

7

     After dinner, Annabelle went to her room to get ready for bed and have a long chat with her best friend, Opie Witherspoon. Opie was Annabelle's bunny rabbit. She would never forget the first moment she saw him at the county fair last fall. She had fallen in love with him the moment she saw his face peering up at her.

     He was the most adorable bunny at the fair. Back then, he'd been no larger than a teacup with black and white spots. His long ears touched the ground when he hopped. He had looked at Annabelle from inside his cage, wiggling his little black nose. Annabelle just couldn't leave him behind.

She spent the rest of that visit to the fair promising to take good care of him. She begged her dad to let her keep him. They were just about to leave the fair when Dad finally gave in.

Opie could always make Annabelle feel better. He would lie beside her, quietly listening as she poured over her day's failures. Annabelle could tell him anything, even about not being able to spell and how much she hated pickle farming. Opie couldn't spell either and disliked pickles as much as Annabelle did. They were the best of friends. They understood each other.

Annabelle changed into her purple pajamas with pink bunnies. She lay on her bed snuggling Opie. She told him about her dreadful day, spelling test, and how long and hard she had studied.

"Opie, I just don't understand why I can't seem to spell. Words just don't look like they sound," Annabelle said, sighing and snuggling closer to her furry friend. "You're so lucky you're a rabbit. You don't ever have to learn to spell."

As Annabelle continued talking, Opie flopped over on his side so that Annabelle could scratch his belly. "Are you more comfortable now?" she asked. Opie just wiggled his nose and closed his eyes. He had grown so much in the past year. He was still small for a lop-eared bunny, but he wouldn't fit into a teacup anymore.

As Annabelle continued to pet and snuggle him, she recalled what her aunt had said.

If everyone has at least one talent, what's mine?

Mom and Dad always told her that she was great at taking care of Mr. Witherspoon. *Was that a talent? What about swinging upside down from the monkey bars?* Maybe that was a talent. Annabelle enjoyed both of them very much, but she didn't know if they would be considered talents.

That night, as she brushed her teeth, she decided that she was going to find out more about her talents. *Thinking about talents is better than thinking about pickles or spelling,* she reasoned. Once in bed, she yawned and quickly fell asleep to dream about swinging upside down.

8

Annabelle yawned so wide that her eyes squeezed shut. She was sitting on her bed, cross-legged, waiting for her aunt's arrival. She had already been up and dressed for hours. The clock on her nightstand showed that it was still early. Annabelle's excitement about spending the summer with her aunt had kept her from sleeping soundly. She had awakened before dawn. This would be her first summer away from home. She couldn't wait for her adventure to begin.

She sat quietly as her thoughts drifted back to her last week of school. She recalled being exhausted after working so hard on her stupid social studies paper. In spite of spending hours sitting on a hard kitchen chair, writing and rewriting her essay, she still received a bad grade. Annabelle recalled the extra spelling test she had to take while her classmates were outside enjoying sunshine. Just like Annabelle had predicted, she failed miserably. Again!

Miss Dunkin had not been pleased. She went so far as to say, "I'm greatly disappointed." *She's disappointed?* thought Annabelle. *Try being me for a day.*

Her memories returned to a happier place when she recalled the surprised looks on her classmates faces. She must have told everyone in her seventh grade class about her summer plans with Aunt Sylvia.

She had even told Molly, the leader of the social club in her class. Molly looked a little jealous when Annabelle talked about her exciting plans. Molly said she would be going to swimming camp for two weeks. Then she would be stuck at home, helping to watch her baby brother for the rest of the summer. No one had ever envied Annabelle before. It almost made her feel normal.

Miss Dunkin suggested that she keep a journal of her summer adventures. Annabelle could read this to the class when school started in the fall.

Uncrossing her legs, Annabelle laughed to herself. *Is Miss Dunkin crazy? She thinks I can write in a journal? The lady must be nuts.* Annabelle wished she could. *Wouldn't it be miraculous to be like everyone else? It must be wonderful to sit down and write about your adventures.*

Annabelle stared out the window. She expected her aunt's car any minute. Her thoughts returned to the last week of school. Nasty Jack hadn't even been able to upset or embarrass her. He tried really hard after her last spelling test. Annabelle kept reminding herself she only had to put up with him for one last test.

She had only gotten two spelling words right out of ten. But she wasn't going to allow her spirits to fall because of another bad spelling test. After all, I'm going to Aunt Sylvia's. She promised to help me find my talents!

"I'm not going to think about journals or spelling," Annabelle said to herself as she moved off the bed and onto the small window seat that overlooked the driveway.

Annabelle tried hard not to dwell on her spelling struggles.

9

Gazing away from the window for a moment, Annabelle checked on Opie. He was sleeping happily in his travel case.

On the floor stood the bright yellow suitcase that she had gotten for her birthday last year. Annabelle had been packed for days. She even had to take one of her shirts out of her suitcase yesterday so that she would have something to wear on her last day of school.

She looked around the room and wondered if she was forgetting anything. She checked to see if she had remembered Opie's favorite chewing blocks and cardboard tunnel. "Yes, it's in my suitcase, along with the special rabbit treat that Mom picked up yesterday," she said.

"She's here! Aunt Sylvia is here! Annabelle, did you hear me? Aunt Sylvia is here!" Emily shouted, sprinting upstairs two at a time and bursting into Annabelle's room.

Emily's excitement startled Annabelle.

She flew to her feet and almost knocked over the flower vase on her nightstand. Rushing into the room, Emily collapsed on the neatly made bed. She paused for a split second to catch her breath. She rolled over to stick her finger into Opie's case.

Opie flinched as Emily's finger came at him. He moved hastily over to the other side of his case. "I can't believe you're not going to help with the pickles this summer," Emily said. "Daddy and I are going to have so much fun. You're going to miss it all." She gave up trying to scratch Opie and pulled her finger back. "Why don't you like picking? How come you're not happy being the daughter of a pickle farmer?"

"I didn't say I didn't want to be the daughter of a pickle farmer!" Annabelle replied. She was astonished by what her little sister said. "I said that I don't like working on a farm. I never said anything about not liking being the daughter of a pickle farmer."

Annabelle rolled her green eyes at Emily and walked over to her suitcase. She lifted the handle and rolled the bag over to the bed. Then she picked up Opie's travel case. Before she left the room, she turned and looked back at her little sister, who was still on her bed.

"I'm glad you love picking pickles and working on a farm. It's not for me. I'm going to spend this summer trying new things. Opie and I are going to have the best summer ever. I want to find things in life that make me happy. Is this hard for you to understand? You enjoy picking pickles, reading books, and playing the piano."

Emily nodded. "I hope you find what makes you happy, Annabelle."

"I hope you know I'll miss you," Annabelle said.

In a flash, Emily leaped off the bed and threw her arms around Annabelle's waist. "I'm going to miss you too," she said, squeezing her tightly.

"Can I carry Opie down to the car for you?" Emily asked as she released her grip around Annabelle's waist and reached for the travel case.

"Yes, but be careful. He doesn't like to be bounced around."

"I will." Emily snatched the case from Annabelle's grip and hurried downstairs with Opie hanging on for dear life.

10

Annabelle awoke as she did every morning, snuggled under her daisy bedspread. Her stomach grumbled. A wonderful smell had woken her up.

What is that delicious odor filling my cozy little bedroom? She yawned and rolled over on her back, licking her lips. *Could it be my favorite breakfast?*

Yes, it was. It was Mom's famous French toast with homemade blueberry syrup!

Annabelle lay there smiling. A ray of sunshine peeked through the daisy-patterned curtains. She could hear familiar sounds drifting upstairs as her family prepared the scrumptious morning meal.

Annabelle's favorite part of the week was the weekend. Any day that wasn't a school day was a good day in her eyes. She got to spend all day with Opie, and she didn't have to see that nasty Jack. Just thinking about him made her face wrinkle up like she had bitten into a sour lemon.

I'm not going to think about school or Jack today. It's the weekend.

Suddenly, she couldn't get out of bed quick enough. She threw back her covers and leaped out of bed. Annabelle decided to dress in her favorite jean shorts and a t-shirt that read, "Be different, don't hop like everyone else!" It had a picture of a rabbit that was using its long ears as legs. Once she was fully dressed, she headed downstairs for breakfast.

As Annabelle strolled into the kitchen, her dad looked up from his chair at the kitchen table.

"There's my early riser," he said as Annabelle came into the kitchen. "I told your mother that the smell of breakfast would entice you to get dressed and come down." He grinned as he put his fork down. Then he pulled out a chair so she could sit beside him.

"Thanks, Dad." Annabelle beamed as she sat down and reached for the platter of French toast.

She was already enjoying her second plate of French toast smothered in blueberry syrup when Emily walked into the kitchen wearing her bib overalls and yellow butterfly t-shirt. Her nose was buried in a book from the local library.

"Emily," Dad said, "I think there's just one thing in this world that you like to do more than work on the farm and that's read. But today, we have a very busy day ahead, so I'm going to need your help. He picked up his fork and finished his last bite.

"But, Daddy, I'm right at the best part. The princess is dancing with the prince, and the fairies are bringing her a big surprise," explained Emily. She began to describe all the fairies and explain why they were bringing the princess the big surprise. She would have told the entire story if Dad hadn't interrupted her when she paused to take a breath.

"Emily, I need you to eat your breakfast!" This time his voice was patient but stern. He gave Emily the "do as you're told" look.

"I only have three more pages to go. Why can't I finish it?" Emily muttered. Hoping to win him over, Emily gave her best puppy-dog eyes look.

Dad chuckled. He couldn't resist tousling her hair as he stood up. "Because you would probably start another book before you finished your breakfast if I didn't stop you now!"

"Oh, okay," she sighed. Emily hurried to the kitchen chair so fast she banged into the table leg, almost spilling Annabelle's milk, causing the book to fall to the floor.

"I'll be ready to go in just two seconds," said Emily, grabbing the serving plate and piling up a stack of French toast.

After pouring almost half a bottle of syrup on her French toast, Emily tried to shovel an entire slice into her mouth.

"Well, you don't have to eat that fast!" laughed Dad. "I have to lace up my work boots and go to the mailbox. You have plenty of time to finish your breakfast. I'll come get you when I'm done."

Annabelle watched with amazement as her sister continued to shovel huge bites into her mouth until Dad returned.

"Come on kid, we have pickles that need us," shouted Dad as he came through the kitchen door.

Emily jumped out of her chair and grabbed her daddy's hand. She loved to spend the entire day with him. As they left the kitchen, Annabelle could hear them chatting about all the farm work they were going to do that day. Annabelle ate her breakfast slowly, looking down at the book that Emily had dropped on the floor.

She wondered why her little sister was so different. Emily enjoyed everything about farming and school. Annabelle liked nothing to do with either. Emily's eagerness to work outside seemed strange to Annabelle. She would rather spend her time completing indoor chores.

Annabelle smiled to herself as she thought, *I'm neat and orderly, and my sister is smart, but she's the biggest slob I've ever seen. For being sisters, we sure are different. I don't think I will ever understand her.*

She reached down and picked up Emily's book.

I know one thing: she really enjoys her fairy tale books, Annabelle thought. *Reading is almost as hard for me as spelling!*

Annabelle went back to eating her breakfast. She dreaded helping with the pickles today.

Those pickles dont need me! I'm just like Aunt Sylvia. I'm just not talented in the art of pickle farming.

A bright idea came to her. Maybe instead of helping outside, she could help Mom in the kitchen today. As she swallowed the last bite of her delicious French toast, she heard her mother call her name.

"Annabelle, when you are done, can you please come in here?"

"Yes, I'm almost done!" Annabelle called back. "I'll be right there." She grabbed her milk, gulped it down in one swallow, and hurried to find her mom.

Annabelle walked into the laundry room where her mother was working.

"Did you feed Opie this morning?" her mother asked.

"Not yet. I have to go outside and pick clover for his breakfast," she explained as she opened the dryer door for her mother.

"That's a very good idea. Your dad and I are very proud of the way you're taking such good care of that rabbit. You have become a very responsible young lady."

"Thanks, Mom. Was that all you wanted?"

"No, it wasn't," her mother began. She pulled a load of towels out of the washer. "Last night, after you went to bed, Dad and I talked about something with Aunt Sylvia. She wondered if you would like to spend the whole summer with her. She believes that the two of you could work on exploring some of your hidden talents. Maybe she could help with your spelling difficulties. What do you think about that, Annabelle?"

Annabelle stood shocked, still holding onto the dryer door. She stared at her mother. It took a second for her to realize what she had just heard. *Is Mom saying I won't have to spend the summer on the farm? I won't have to touch those green prickly pickles the entire summer? This has to be a dream! No pickles for Annabelle?*

Annabelle could only think of one thing to ask. "When can I go, Mom? I can have my suitcase and Opie packed in two minutes," she said excitedly. She didn't want to take the chance that her parents would change their minds.

"You have to finish your last week of school first," Mom laughed. She hadn't seen Annabelle this happy in a very long time. She watched her daughter jump around the laundry room with excitement.

"Ok, I can do that! Then I get to go to Aunt Sylvia's house next weekend, right?"

"Yes," was all her mom managed to say before Annabelle ran out of the room yelling.

"I have to go tell Opie!" she shouted excitedly back to her mother. "This is going to be the best summer ever! No pickles for me! No pickles for Opie! No pickles forever, at least not for this summer!"

Annabelle's mom stood smiling to herself in the doorway as she watched her daughter run upstairs to share the news with her rabbit. She loved her daughter so much and had been worried about how quiet and withdrawn she had become lately.

"I hope Annabelle can find her hidden talents," she said to herself. "It took me a long time too." Turning her attention back to the dryer, she pushed the start button, and the cycle began.

No Pickles for Annabelle

11

      Opie Witherspoon sat in his traveling case on Annabelle's lap. Annabelle looked calm as she sat quietly in Aunt Sylvia's car. On the inside, though, she was dancing with excitement as Aunt Sylvia's sporty little black car zipped down the interstate. She desperately wanted to tell her aunt how grateful she was. She couldn't find the right words to describe her feelings. She wanted to shout at the top of her lungs, "I'm free! I'm free from school and pickles!" But she didn't. Annabelle just sat quietly smiling, wearing her sunglasses, and holding her rabbit's traveling case.

Unfortunately, Opie wasn't as confident as Annabelle. He sat up on his back haunches and looked cautiously through the vent in his case. His ears were up and his nose moved rapidly. Opie Witherspoon wasn't happy about leaving his home.

Annabelle leaned down to comfort Opie. His terrified black eyes stared up at her. "It's okay," she said in a consoling voice. She heard him grunt. "I'm right here. We're going to Aunt Sylvia's house, remember? You've been there before."

Carefully, Annabelle opened the top of the case and reached in to reassure him with a pat. After hearing her voice and feeling her touch, Opie began to calm down. He moved nearer to Annabelle's hand and gave it a little lick. Then, he nudged himself closer so that she could rub behind his ears better.

"That's a good bunny. You just needed some attention, didn't you?" Annabelle asked tenderly.

She looked up to watch the freshly plowed farmland zoom by her window. Annabelle couldn't stop grinning, knowing that she wouldn't have any part of this year's pickle crop.

Aunt Sylvia glanced over at Annabelle. "We are going to have so much fun this summer," she said with a big smile on her face. "I just know we're going to find that you have lots of hidden talents."

"I hope so," Annabelle answered. "If we don't, it will still be okay. I get to spend the summer away from those nasty prickly pickles." She hoped her aunt could hear the gratitude in her voice.

Aunt Sylvia laughed and smiled. "I think we can find at least one talent this summer," she said. "So tell me, what makes you happy?"

"Well," Annabelle replied as she squirmed uneasily in her seat. Her fingers started to nervously fiddle with the metal lock on the cage.

Looking down at her pink flip-flops, she said, "I like Opie. He makes me happy."

"I can see that." Aunt Sylvia laughed, looking toward the rabbit's case. "I believe Opie would say that you make him very happy, too."

"I also like playing dress-up, decorating my bedroom,and singing. Oh, and cooking with Mom is fun."

"Is there anything that makes you the happiest?" asked Aunt Sylvia.

"Yes, but you'll think it's silly."

"No I won't," replied her aunt. "If you like doing something, then I would love to know what I is."

"Okay. I love to swing while I'm hanging upside-down."

"That sounds like fun," her aunt said taking her eyes off the road for just a second to look at Annabelle. "Have you ever watched other people swing upside down?" she asked.

"No," replied Annabelle.

"Have you always loved to swing upside down?" Aunt Sylvia asked.

"Yes, for as long as I can remember," Annabelle said with a faraway look in her eyes.

Aunt Sylvia drove quietly for a few moments as her thoughts made her smooth forehead wrinkle up above her sharp blue eyes. Aunt Sylvia grinned. "I think I know just the place to go." Soon they turned off the interstate and were headed away from town.

12

A short time later, Annabelle felt the car slow down as her aunt turned off the asphalt road into a small gravel parking lot. Annabelle stopped petting Opie and looked up as she heard the sound of tires crunching through gravel.

"Are we there?" she asked excitedly, looking out the window.

"Yes, we are."

Annabelle rolled down the window to see a large yellow and blue sign on a white striped building. The only word on the sign that caught her eye was "School."

"What are we doing here?" Annabelle gasped. She couldn't believe her aunt had brought her to a school! She felt betrayed. *Doesn't she know that school is over for the summer? Doesn't she understand that I hate school?* Annabelle had no interest in stepping one foot inside this place! For a moment, she thought about planting her feet against the floorboard and refusing to get out.

Aunt Sylvia must've seen the confusion on her face. "Aren't you coming?" she asked as she opened her door and stepped out.

Aunt Sylvia stood patiently holding the front passenger door open so Annabelle could get out. Annabelle was looking straight down at the floor. Her mind was racing and her heart was pounding. She had to think fast. Annabelle fought back tears as she said, "I can't leave Opie in the car. It's too hot for him."

"I know Opie can't stay in the car. You can bring him with us," Aunt Sylvia smiled. "I'll even carry him in for you."

And just like that, Aunt Sylvia grabbed the case and headed for the entrance. Any possibility of escaping had vanished. Aunt Sylvia had taken her bunny. She was expected to follow. Annabelle reluctantly stepped out of the car, shuffling her feet, which created a cloud of dust around her.

"What kind of place is this?" Annabelle mumbled, still trying to find a way out of this horrible predicament.

"It's a place for people who love to hang upside down and swing. They come here to have fun."

"They do?" Annabelle glanced over at her aunt, deeply skeptical. Was there really a place for people like her, for people who liked to hang upside down? "But the sign says it's a school," she ventured. "I don't understand."

"Yes, it's a circus school," Aunt Sylvia explained. "It's a place where people of all ages come to learn how to be jugglers, acrobats, clowns, or tight-wire walkers."

"And lion tamers?" Annabelle asked as she began to feel a small wave of relief.

"No, I don't think they teach lion taming," Aunt Sylvia answered with a serious look on her face. "Why? Do you want to be a lion tamer?"

"No, I don't think Opie would get along very well with a lion," Annabelle giggled.

"I think you're right, Annabelle. You'd better stick to trapeze art."

"What's trapeze art?"

Aunt Sylvia smiled down at Annabelle. "Trapeze artists are people who perform acrobatic tricks very high in the air over a large net. They begin by climbing to a high platform and grabbing a trapeze bar held by two large ropes from the ceiling. Then, they jump off the platform, letting their body swing back and forth while hanging upside down. Next, the trapeze artist lets go and someone swinging from the other side catches them. When the trick is completed, the trapeze artist lets go and falls safely onto the net below."

Annabelle was frozen with a mixture of disbelief and excitement as she listened to her aunt's description.

"Annabelle," her aunt continued, "this school teaches kids how to become trapeze artists. Shall we go inside and see if we can sign up for a class?"

Aunt Sylvia now had Annabelle's full attention! She couldn't believe she was going back to school for the summer . . . not just any old school, but a school that would teach her how to swing upside down and fly through the air. She was going to become a trapeze artist! Excited, Annabelle quickened her pace. She wanted to catch up to her aunt so they could enter together.

Annabelle and her aunt walked hand-in-hand as they entered through a creaky, wooden door. Inside, a teenage girl with long, straight black hair was standing behind a counter.

"Welcome," she greeted them, flashing a friendly smile. "My name's Jasmine. May I help you?"

"Yes, you may." Aunt Sylvia smiled back. She sat Opie down on the floor beside her feet. "My niece would like to sign up for your trapeze classes."

Aunt Sylvia glanced down and pulled Annabelle to her side, giving her a little squeeze.

"I can help with that," said the girl, nodding as she leaned down. She pulled out a few forms from under the counter and handed them to Aunt Sylvia.

"Are you a trapeze artist?" Annabelle asked shyly as she removed her yellow sunglasses.

"Yes, I am and also a tight-wire artist, but my passion is flying aerial silk."

Annabelle had heard of tight-wire but not flying aerial silk. She decided she would have to ask. "I beg your pardon, but what does a flying aerial silk person do?"

Jasmine explained, "Flying silk is when a performer hangs by special fabric and performs acrobatic tricks. I wrap the fabric around myself and do things like swings and suspended falls. My body spirals into and out of various positions. Aerial silks is athleticism and flexibility all rolled into one."

"How far up in the air are you?" Annabelle asked, astonished. Her eyes looked up to the high ceiling.

"Most flying aerial silk artists perform their routine about twenty to thirty-four feet in the air. Some of the performers are practicing now. You can go down the hall and have a look at them if you want." Jasmine pointed with her bright pink fingernail toward a long corridor.

"Can I, Aunt Sylvia? Can I go see the performers?" Annabelle asked with more enthusiasm than her aunt had ever seen from her.

"I think that would be an excellent idea," Aunt Sylvia laughed as she began to spread out the forms on the counter top. "You go enjoy yourself. I'll be busy here for a while, signing you up for classes."

Before Aunt Sylvia could say another word, Annabelle was gone. She ran down the hall as fast as her legs would carry her.

The closer she got to the end of the hallway, the louder the sounds became. She heard metal striking metal and loud voices booming out commands. She could also hear other voices laughing and giggling. She even heard cheers and clapping sounds.

She came to an abrupt stop at an open doorway at the end of the hallway. Peering in, Annabelle couldn't believe her eyes! The biggest gym she had ever seen was swarming with kids.

Some of them were hanging upside down from the ceiling!

Two girls were hanging from a large metal ring doing acrobatic tricks. As she turned her head, she saw a man riding a bike with three girls who were her own age. Two of the girls were standing on the handlebars. One was seated on the man's shoulders. This was one of the most peculiar things that Annabelle had ever seen!

As she moved farther inside the gym, her eyes drifted up to the ceiling. There she spotted a lady in a brightly colored costume flying through the air, holding on to a large metal bar. Meanwhile, a man on the other side of the room was hanging upside down from another metal bar. His arms were outstretched toward the brightly clothed lady.

Annabelle watched in awe. Her eyes widened as the lady let go of the bar she had been swinging on. She successfully completed a back flip in midair before the man hanging upside-down caught her. In stunned silence, Annabelle stared as the man dropped the lady, letting her fall into a huge net. The lady bounced onto her back like a beach ball.

Flying through the air like that must be so cool!

As she turned her attention away from the lady in the net, she spotted the aerial silk performers in the back of the room. They reminded her of flying ballerinas. Annabelle had never seen anything so graceful. She watched them swing in and out of the silk fabric, slowly descending until they reached the ground. Several of the silk artists who had reached the floor were now doing some flexibility exercises.

Annabelle continued to gaze at the remaining areas of the gym.

She spotted people bouncing high into the air on trampolines. Others were doing acrobatics on a blue mat. She was astonished to see two people on bikes gliding across a wire stretched through the air.

Annabelle couldn't take it in all at once! At that moment, all she knew was that she didn't ever want to leave this heavenly place. She had always felt that she wasn't the smartest kid in her classroom. When she and other kids teamed up to play games during recess, she was always one of the last kids chosen. Rarely did Annabelle feel like she fit in. But here, in this place, she felt like she belonged. She was with people just like her.

"I love circus school!" was all Annabelle could say.

She couldn't believe she said the words "school" and "love" in the same sentence. She quickly turned around and ran back to find her aunt. She wanted to tell her every marvelous detail of what she had just seen.

13

Annabelle strained her neck to watch the circus school shrink from view through the back window of her aunt's car.

"I can't believe I have to wait until Monday," she sighed as she turned back around.

"I know," agreed Aunt Sylvia, looking from the road to her niece, "but it's only two days away. Before you know it, it'll be Monday."

"I hope so," sighed Annabelle as she laid her head against the window.

"Why don't we get you and Opie settled in at my place?" said Aunt Sylvia. "I can show you what I've done to my guest bedroom for you and Opie."

Aunt Sylvia drove her sporty little black car onto the interstate and headed for her house.

After the excitement of the circus school, the drive to Aunt Sylvia's house was quiet. While Opie slept in his travel case, Annabelle was lost in her thoughts.

Aunt Sylvia was right. The weekend would go by quickly. Monday was just around the corner.

Later that night, Annabelle was snuggling with Opie in bed. She heard a soft knock on the bedroom door.

"Come in," she called. Aunt Sylvia was carrying a white wooden tray of homemade brownies and two large glasses of milk.

"Wow!" Annabelle exclaimed. She sat up to put Opie on the hardwood floor beside her bed. Opie proceeded to stretch his ears, and then he quickly darted under the bed to continue his nap.

"Those sure look good!" Annabelle grinned. Seeing the brownies made her taste buds tingle in anticipation.

"I hope they taste as good as they look," offered Aunt Sylvia. She put the tray on the flowered bedspread.

"I was thinking this would be a good time to talk about some things I have planned for you this summer," she added. She joined Annabelle and the tray on the crowded bed. Aunt Sylvia picked up a brownie and took a bite.

"Okay," Annabelle replied as she picked up a brownie, trying not to spill crumbs. "I don't care what we do, as long as it's not picking those prickly pickles." She bit into the warm, chewy brownie.

Aunt Sylvia laughed. "I hope you still feel the same way after I explain other plans I have for this summer," she said. "I would like to talk to you about your spelling. I know you don't like to talk about your difficulties in school. I think you need someone to help you. I think I'm perfect for the job."

Annabelle's cheerful expression turned into a look of panic. Her aunt's words sent her stomach plummeting. Just hearing the word "spelling" caused a tidal wave of nausea. Her body became so limp that she almost let the brownie fall from her hand. Quickly, she thought to place it back on the tray.

Her family had tried, countless times, to convince her that she needed to try harder and study more. They told her if she would pay closer attention in class and stay focused she would "get it."

But none of their suggestions made any difference. Now, Aunt Sylvia was going to team up with them against her. *Doesn't anyone understand how hard it is for me?*

Annabelle thought quickly. She needed to distract her aunt from the subject of spelling. "Aunt Sylvia," she smiled, "can we go shopping tomorrow? I think I'll need some more Timothy hay for Opie." Annabelle smiled even wider as she continued. "Did you know bunnies need to have plenty of hay to eat? Eating the hay helps to keep their teeth ground down. If bunnies don't keep their teeth ground down, they can grow so long that they can't eat at all!"

Aunt Sylvia grinned and nodded. "That's very interesting, Annabelle," she said. "I'd love to hear more about caring for bunnies. First, we need to talk about getting you some help with your spelling. I'd like to ask you a few questions. All you have to do is answer honestly."

Annabelle's mind was racing. She couldn't lie to her aunt; that would be wrong. But she couldn't truly be honest with her either! She couldn't risk losing her aunt's respect and love. She didn't know what to do.

What if Aunt Sylvia finds out that I try hard and I still can't spell? She'll think I'm dumb just like the kids at school do!

She realized there was no escape from this conversation. She looked at her lap. The first tear slid down her cheek.

"I just have a few simple questions, Annabelle." Aunt Sylvia spoke tenderly as she wiped the tear from her niece's cheek. "I want to understand why you hate spelling so much. I want to find out if there's anything I can do to help. Is it alright if I ask?"

"I guess so," Annabelle mumbled, refusing to look up.

"Okay," Aunt Sylvia started, "here is the first question. When you think of an idea in your head, is it easier to talk about the idea or to put the idea down on paper?"

Annabelle thought about her answer for a few moments before answering. "Talk. I don't like to write because I can't spell all the words," she said. She expected to hear disappointment in Aunt Sylvia's voice, but it didn't come.

Maybe she didn't hear me.

"So talking is easier for you," repeated her aunt. She gently moved a strand of hair from Annabelle's face, then tucked it behind her ear. "Here's the next question. Does anyone ever laugh at things you say, but you don't understand what they're laughing about?"

"Sometimes," Annabelle said. "Sometimes they say I talk funny."

Again, Annabelle waited for her aunt to call her dumb. Again, there were no nasty remarks or looks.

"You're doing very well, Annabelle," her aunt said. She even picked up Annabelle's brownie and handed it back to her. "I only have a few more questions."

"Okay," Annabelle said solemnly. She still felt panicky, but the nausea and urge to cry were starting to pass.

"Do you have trouble copying words or letters? Has anyone ever told you that some of your letters are backwards? Or do they say they can't read your handwriting?"

"No," Annabelle said with a little spark of pride in her voice. She didn't mind questions about her handwriting. "I'm good at copying words. Miss Dunkin, my teacher, said my penmanship is very good."

"I'm so glad to hear that," Aunt Sylvia smiled cheerfully. "We're almost done. You're doing so well! Thanks for being so honest."

"It's okay," Annabelle said, but she didn't mean it. She didn't feel okay. Just like when she had to take the weekly spelling test, she felt she didn't have a choice. She hoped Aunt Sylvia wouldn't want to talk about this every week.

"When you try to sound out a word, do some letters sound the same as others?" asked Aunt Sylvia.

"Yes," Annabelle answered, "they do. My teacher says I'm just not saying them right. I don't understand what she means, though."

"This is the last question, Annabelle," said Aunt Sylvia.

Finally!

"If I could help you understand why you're having trouble and help you improve your spelling, would you like that?"

Annabelle turned her head and looked at her aunt with red, swollen eyes.

"Don't you understand? I can't! I try and try, but I still can't spell. I'm just dumb!" With that, Annabelle threw herself face down on the bed and began to sob.

"Annabelle," said her aunt, as she leaned over and rubbed Annabelle's back. "You are not dumb! You are one of the smartest, most talented, most awesome young ladies I know!"

"You're just saying that," Annabelle sobbed into her pillow.

"Annabelle, sweetheart, you need to listen to me. Everyone learns in their own way and at their own speed."

"They do?" asked Annabelle, still burying her face into the pillow.

"Yes, just because you have problems with spelling does not mean you're dumb. It may just mean you learn differently. I learn differently, too."

Annabelle turned her head just enough to see her aunt.

"Yes, honey, I believe you just learn differently than most of your classmates."

"How do you know?"

"I know because I'm an educational therapist."

"A what?" asked Annabelle, puzzled.

"An educational therapist is someone who works with children who learn differently, just like you. Remember last week, when I visited you?"

"Yes," she replied as she tried to steady her voice. She wiped her tear-stained cheek with the back of her hand and slowly turned to face her aunt.

"Your mom and dad invited me over to discuss your spelling difficulties. They're worried about you. They know something can be done to help you. So tomorrow, we're going to discover different ways for you to learn."

"I'd like that," Annabelle leaned her head against her aunt's shoulder. She wasn't alone anymore. Someone finally understood.

"Me too," Aunt Sylvia sighed, kissing the top of Annabelle's head.

"Now let's finish our snack. You can help me clean up the kitchen."

"Sounds good to me," Annabelle said as she took another bite of her brownie.

14

Sunlight streamed through the branches of a large, old maple tree. It provided sunshine for Aunt Sylvia's prized daisy flowerbed. Aunt Sylvia stood watching her niece swing upside down from her knees on one of the branches. The sunlight shimmered on Annabelle's hair.

"Annabelle, can you come inside for a moment?" she called through the screen door. "I have something for you."

"Okay," Annabelle replied. She grabbed the tree branch with both hands to let herself down.

Aunt Sylvia smiled as she watched her let go and drop, feet first, to the ground. "You sure do enjoy hanging upside down, don't you?" Aunt Sylvia said.

"I do! Hanging upside down is my favorite activity," Annabelle beamed as she hurried toward the door. "Would you like to hang upside down with me? It's so much fun, and everything looks so different. You'd love it!

"I'll make a deal with you. I'll come hang upside down with you, if you'll let me help you with your spelling first."

Annabelle's face wrinkled up as though she smelled dirty gym shoes. "Do I have to?" Annabelle protested with a groan.

"Yes, you do," insisted her aunt. "But before we start, I have a present for you."

"A present for me?" asked Annabelle.

Aunt Sylvia stretched out her hand with the present and explained, "You may not understand why I picked out this particular present for you, but remember, I believe you can do anything!"

"Can I open it?"

"Yes," Aunt Sylvia laughed, "let's go open it at the kitchen table."

Annabelle couldn't take her eyes off the polka-dotted wrapping paper. She followed her aunt into the kitchen.

Sitting at the small breakfast table, Annabelle eagerly ripped open the present. As the last piece of wrapping paper fell on the floor, she sat staring at a little pink book. She didn't know what to say. It was a book of empty pages.

"Do you like it?" Aunt Sylvia asked. "I saw it in the store last week. I just knew it would be perfect for you. Isn't pink your favorite color?"

"Yes, pink is my favorite color." Annabelle stared at the empty book in her hands. She was silent for a moment. She tried to hide her disappointment. She continued, "Thank you so much for buying me a present. I really like it." Secretly Annabelle didn't know what she would do with this useless book.

"I was thinking," explained Aunt Sylvia, "that you could keep a journal this summer about all the new, exciting adventures you're going to have."

"But Aunt Sylvia," Annabelle said with frustration, "my thoughts and feelings may be screaming to get out, but nothing has changed since last night." Annabelle looked down at the present. She still couldn't spell.

Unfortunately, her aunt didn't seem to understand. She just smiled and told Annabelle to keep the book. Maybe she would change her mind.

"Maybe," Annabelle said, trying to sound more upbeat than she felt. She wanted to please her aunt, but knew the book would never be used.

Aunt Sylvia leaned toward Annabelle, tenderly squeezing her niece's slender, drooped shoulder. "I know you are discouraged right now." She smiled into Annabelle's sad green eyes. When their eyes met, she continued. "I guarantee spelling will get easier by the end of summer. Do you trust me?"

Annabelle thought for a moment. "Yes," Annabelle said, mustering as much enthusiasm as she could.

Aunt Sylvia reached over to the counter, picked up an intimidating-looking book, and flipped through the first few pages.

"Well, let's get started with your evaluation, so I can go outside and try hanging upside down," Aunt Sylvia said with a grin.

"All right," said Annabelle reluctantly. She didn't really want to have any part in this evaluation. Fearful, she shifted her weight and moved the blank journal over. She prepared herself for another humiliating experience.

Aunt Sylvia opened up the important-looking book. She explained that the evaluation would last for one hour. After it was complete, they would talk about what they had discovered. They could continue to improve Annabelle's understanding of her spelling difficulties throughout the summer.

Aunt Sylvia reminded Annabelle that everyone has strengths and weaknesses when they are learning.

"I bet Jack doesn't have any weakness," sighed Annabelle, looking down at her present.

"Is Jack a classmate?" asked Aunt Sylvia.

"Yes, he's a horrible boy in my class. He always makes fun of me and tells everyone how bad I do on my spelling tests. He thinks he knows everything, and I hate him!"

"It doesn't sound like Jack knows how to be nice," said Aunt Sylvia. "That's something you're very good at. There are probably some things at school that Jack doesn't understand. Some kids learn differently than other kids. Some kids even feel like they don't fit in with the other kids at school."

She went on to say those same kids feel like they would rather stay in bed with their blankets pulled over their heads than face another school day.

Annabelle could relate to those kids. Annabelle remembered all the times she had tried to convince her mother that she didn't feel good, so that she wouldn't have to face a spelling test.

Aunt Sylvia went on. "Did you know that people can be smart in many different ways?"

Annabelle shook her head.

"First, there's word-smart. If you're word-smart, that means you're good at using words to talk, read, or write. Then there's music-smart, which means you're good at singing or playing a musical instrument. There's also number-smart. If you're number-smart, you might be good at math, riddles, or even computers."

As Annabelle listened, she began to realize that maybe she wasn't as dumb as she had always thought. "I must be number-smart. Even Miss Dunkin called me smart when I got a one hundred on my math test," said Annabelle.

Aunt Sylvia continued, "Some people are body-smart. That means their body is really good at following directions, so they are great at moving their body any way they want."

"I'm great at moving my body around on the monkey bars and the swing! I must be body-smart, too," said Annabelle.

"People who are picture-smart are really good at noticing details, so they are great at drawing and designing things," said her aunt. "Another way of being smart is self-smart or people-smart. People who are smart in that way are really good at understanding themselves and other people."

"And finally," said Aunt Sylvia, "there is nature-smart. People who are nature-smart might enjoy things like animals, plants, gardening, or cooking."

"I'm nature-smart too," Annabelle realized. "Nature-smart people enjoy animals and cooking. I love Opie, and I like cooking with Mom."

"Yes!" Aunt Sylvia said. "I think you're talented in numbers, body, and nature. I also believe that you're smart in all eight. Just because you might have trouble spelling doesn't mean that you're not smart. It just means that you may be smarter in other areas."

"So why can't I spell?" Annabelle asked.

"I don't know yet," her aunt said, "but we're going to find out together. What I do know is that it's not your fault. You didn't do anything wrong. Some people are just born this way," her aunt continued. "It doesn't make you any less smart. It just means you're different. In fact, it makes you unique!"

Annabelle had never heard anyone say such nice things about her before. *Could her aunt be right? Could she really be smart and talented?* She realized that she was looking forward to receiving help from her aunt. She was finally going to understand why she couldn't spell very well. She still might not be the best speller in her room next year, but maybe that was okay. Aunt Sylvia said she was smart in all eight areas. She was even talented in three!

Aunt Sylvia and Annabelle worked hard most of the afternoon. When the testing was completed, they talked about Annabelle's strengths and weaknesses.

They discussed ways to help her become a better speller.

Eventually, Aunt Sylvia said they were finished working. As Annabelle stood up from the kitchen table, she grinned at her aunt. "Aunt Sylvia, time to come outside and learn how to hang upside down!"

15

"Attention! Attention, class!" shouted the two instructors. "Can everyone gather round, please?" They moved toward a large blue safety mat lying in the corner of the room. Annabelle's trapeze classmates hurried eagerly over to where the instructors were standing.

Annabelle slowly took off her sneakers and socks. She was uncertain as she moved toward the giggling group. Her doubts about herself and her abilities came rushing back.

What if I can't do it? It's awfully high! I bet everyone will be better than me. I'm not a trapeze artist; I'm just a girl who likes to swing upside down.

She paused, and then she muttered, "I don't think I can do this!"

"Did you say something to me?" asked an energetic girl standing next to her. She looked about the same age as Annabelle.

Annabelle had been so distracted by her own thoughts she hadn't even noticed someone standing so close.

"No," said Annabelle sheepishly.

"Oh, I thought you said, 'I don't think I can do this,'" said the girl. She had blue eyes and a freckled nose. Annabelle noticed that she was wearing a butterfly headband that held back thick, blonde hair.

"It's my first day," admitted Annabelle. "I'm not sure what I'm supposed to be doing."

"I bet you'll be brilliant!" the young girl said, as she threw her arms up in the air. She beamed from ear to ear. "If you like, you can sit by me. My name is Haley. I was here last year. I loved it so much that I couldn't wait to come back."

Haley tipped her head back and closed her eyes. She began to spin as if she were already on the trapeze. The faster she spun, the more she giggled. Her infectious giggles caused her to collapse at Annabelle's feet.

Seeing Haley giggling on the floor helped Annabelle relax. "Yes, let's definitely sit together," Annabelle agreed. She was happy to find someone to make her feel welcome.

Haley let out a high-pitched squeal. She grabbed Annabelle's hand as she gasped, "We'd better hurry if we want to get a good spot at the front of the class!"

And just like that, Annabelle had made her first best friend. Well, her first best friend who wasn't a rabbit.

Annabelle and Haley sat crossed-legged on the foam mat while the two instructors checked attendance. Annabelle looked around and saw kids of all ages. There were several her age, a few older, and even some younger kids. They were hanging on every word the instructors were saying.

The two instructors' names were Jeremy and Zach. Jeremy was tall with curly brown hair. He didn't seem to like smiling. Zach was shorter with black hair and big brown eyes.

First, Jeremy talked about all of the different safety rules, including the safety belt that everyone had to wear. He talked about paying special attention to all the instructors.

As Annabelle listened, she started to feel more excited about becoming a trapeze artist.

Zach stood up and told the students how to properly prepare for the high trapeze bar. They would begin by hanging from their hands and then by their knees, using only the lower bar. He turned and pointed to the short metal bars standing to one side of the room. All of the students turned their heads and looked in the direction he pointed.

They watched Jeremy demonstrate using the lower bar.

"Whew, that sounds like a good idea," Annabelle whispered to Haley. "I don't think I'd like being up so high on the first day."

"You'll love it once you do it," Haley assured her. Annabelle looked up toward the narrow ladder that leaned against the black platform. Their instructors had informed them the platform was over thirty feet high.

The girls turned their attention back to Zach. He stated, "Until every student masters the lower practice bar, no one will be going to the high bar. We will assist each student through a routine on the lower bar. This will allow each of you to feel the different ways your body needs to move. It's easier to learn without being up so high."

When both instructors were finished talking, the students moved over to the low bar. Jeremy demonstrated the routine each student would have to learn. Next, he taught them the proper way to climb the narrow ladder. Then, they learned the correct way to hold the trapeze bar and how to do the big jump.

Annabelle and her classmates spent most of the morning practicing with the low bar.

"You're doing really well!" Haley said excitedly to Annabelle. "You look like you've been doing this for years."

"I think I was born hanging upside down and swinging," Annabelle said, laughing as she swung. "This is the kind of school I could learn to love."

"Me too," agreed Haley.

As they continued to talk, they heard Zach yell to the class to line up.

"Why do we have to line up?" asked Annabelle. She didn't want to get down off the bar.

"I think it's time to go on the high bar!" Haley replied with excitement.

Both girls ran toward Zach, hand in hand.

16

Annabelle stood in line, waiting for her turn. She spotted her aunt entering the gym. Aunt Sylvia smiled at Annabelle as she sat on the bleachers to watch.

One at a time, Annabelle's classmates climbed the narrow ladder to the platform. When it was her turn, Annabelle's heart pounded with excitement. In her mind, she reviewed the instructions she had received. She pictured herself standing on the platform with her toes curled over the edge. Her right hand should hold the trapeze bar and her left should grasp the metal post on the platform. She pictured herself letting go of the post, firmly grabbing the bar with both hands. She imagined hearing the instructor yelling, "Go!" She could hardly wait!

"Annabelle!" shouted Zach from the platform. "Are you ready? Let's get you flying."

Hearing her name brought Annabelle back to reality. "Yes," Annabelle called back. She put chalk on her hands and arms just like the instructors had taught her. Then, she began climbing the tall ladder. She looked over at her aunt and smiled. Then she looked down at Haley. Haley had just taken her turn and was climbing down from the net.

"You were great! I hope I'm as good as you were," called Annabelle.

"You'll be brilliant!" Haley shouted back, grinning at her friend.

When Annabelle reached the platform, Zach fastened the safety belt around her waist, pulling on the strap to make sure it was snug.

"This will keep you safe and help the other instructor on the ground guide you throughout your swing," Zach said as he double-checked his work.

Next, Zach showed Annabelle one more time where to properly place her feet. Zach reached down for the trapeze bar with a large metal hook and hauled it up to the platform.

"Here, Annabelle. Grab the fly bar with your left hand," Zach said.

As Zach had instructed, Annabelle grasped the bar in her left hand. The bar felt cold in her hand, and she was surprised by how heavy it was.

"Now, take your right hand off the platform pole, and grab hold of your trapeze bar with both hands. Hold on tight."

Annabelle did as she was told. She was now holding the fly bar with both hands. Her heart raced with excitement.

"Annabelle, I need you to lean forward and arch your back a little more," Zach told her. He nudged her just a little bit. "You got it," Zach smiled, giving Annabelle a thumbs-up sign.

Annabelle grinned. Zach stood behind her and held onto the safety ropes.

"Are you ready Annabelle?" Zach asked.

She knew she was ready. She was poised, her feet curled over the edge. She was firmly holding the trapeze bar. This was a dream come true. She felt she had been ready for years.

"I'm ready!" she said.

"Then jump!" Zach yelled.

Annabelle leapt off the platform as if she had been flying all of her life. The wind rushed past her as she felt the weight of her body pull on her arms. Her hands automatically tightened around the bar. Annabelle was swinging higher and faster than she had ever swung before.

"I'm flying!" she squealed to the small group of onlookers standing around the safety net.

Still beaming from ear to ear, Annabelle could feel herself begin to swing back toward the starting platform. She heard Zach call, "Legs up!"

Annabelle was surprised at how little momentum was really needed to swing her legs up over the bar. As she hooked the bar behind her knees, she wondered if she looked like a spider monkey at the zoo.

She was now ready for the next instruction from Zach.

On the next swing, the instruction was, "Arms down!" Again, she followed directions and dropped her arms. She was swinging upside down, hanging from her knees thirty feet above the ground.

Annabelle knew from that morning's practice that after she dropped her arms, she needed to arch her back and reach over her head. She also needed to make sure she could see Jeremy, who would be swinging toward her. She arched her back and spotted Jeremy swinging toward her. She focused on his hands and heard him call out, "Grab my arms, Annabelle." Just as they were within reach of one another, she grabbed Jeremy's arms and he grabbed hers. They were locked together.

"Unhook now," Jeremy instructed. Annabelle unhooked her legs. She felt her lower body drop and realized she was hanging from her instructors arms.

Wow, I'm really flying! This is the coolest feeling and the most fun I've ever had in my whole life!

While hanging from Jeremy's firm grip, she looked down and spotted her aunt beaming up at her.

"Look at me!" Annabelle shouted triumphantly.

One last swing across the net and Jeremy shouted, "Release me!" At the same time, he released her, and she dropped safely onto the net. The landing was surprisingly soft.

Still following the instructions received during practice, Annabelle quickly sat up and bounced to the side of the net. She grasped the edge of the net and rolled over, gracefully landing on the mat below.

Annabelle's knees were still shaking with excitement as all of her classmates crowded around her.

"You looked great!" Haley squealed, hugging her and beaming. "And you got it your very first try!"

"Do you think they'll let me go again?" Annabelle asked, still breathing hard from all the excitement.

"They only let us go once today," Haley said, letting go of Annabelle. She leaned over to pick up her gym bag. "I have to run. My mom is waiting in the car."

"Ok," Annabelle said as she waved goodbye to her new friend. "See you tomorrow!"

Zach grinned at Annabelle as he walked toward her. "You have a real talent for this," he said. "We're so delighted you joined our summer trapeze class." He patted her on the back. "I think you're a real natural."

Annabelle's mouth dropped open as she gazed into her instructor's smiling face.

"Am I?" Annabelle asked, blushing. "I didn't think I could do it. I was so nervous."

Annabelle looked over at her classmates stretching out on the mats. No one had ever thought she was a natural at anything before. She felt slightly embarrassed but proud.

"Well, you didn't look nervous to me. If you keep working as hard as you did today, you're going to be performing amazing routines by the end of the summer."

"I am?" Annabelle said. "I love it here!" she blurted out. It was the only thing she could think to say.

Zach chuckled and nodded his head as Aunt Sylvia came strolling over to them.

"Bravo! You did a fabulous job!" Aunt Sylvia said. She hugged Annabelle. "I'm so proud of you!"

"I'm proud of me, too," Annabelle admitted. "I can't believe I have to wait until tomorrow to do it again." She raised her arms above her head. She began to spin gracefully, recalling the sensation of flying through the air.

"I know. It's a long time until tomorrow, but that gives us time to find more of your hidden talents," Aunt Sylvia laughed.

"That's true," Annabelle remarked. Suddenly, she stopped mid-spin to look over at her aunt. She had forgotten to tell Aunt Sylvia the best part!

"Did you hear that Zach said I had a talent as a trapeze artist? Me! A trapeze artist! I have a talent!" She began to twirl around the gym. "Maybe someday I'll be famous!"

Aunt Sylvia watched her niece dance around the room. She realized just how much she was going to enjoy helping her niece find her hidden talents.

"Annabelle," she said, still smiling, "don't forget about your other talents. Remember the ones we talked about last night? Remember the talent for caring for Opie Witherspoon?"

"Yes, that's right, two talents," Annabelle said holding up two fingers in the air.

"And did you forget about your other talent?"

"What other talent?" Annabelle asked, stopping abruptly to push the hair off her face.

"Your talent for numbers," Aunt Sylvia replied.

"Oh, that's right. I totally forgot about that one! Hey, Zach, did you know that I have three talents?" Annabelle exclaimed, dancing back to where he and Aunt Sylvia stood.

"I bet you have a lot more than three," Zach replied, smiling at Annabelle. "I bet you'll find you have dozens of talents." Zach leaned over and hugged her. He smiled and waved as he walked away, saying, "See you tomorrow, Annabelle."

"Did you hear what he said?" Annabelle turned to look at her aunt. "He thinks I might have dozens of talents. Do you think he could be right?"

"Yes, I do. And won't it be great fun finding them?"

"Yes!" agreed Annabelle. "I can't wait!"

"Me either!" Aunt Sylvia replied. "Now let's go home, so you can tell Opie about your exciting day. Let's celebrate your new-found talents."

As Annabelle left the circus school, she barely heard all the compliments of "great job" or "nice work." She suddenly realized that she had talents!

She had finally figured it out. She didn't have to be the best at spelling or reading. Annabelle knew it would have been nice if she were talented in spelling and reading like her classmates or little sister. But she wasn't, and that was okay. Just because she had a difficult time learning at school didnt mean she wasn't talented in other ways. All that really mattered was that she tried to do her best. She finally understood that everyone's talents were unique to them. She was talented in her own way.

As Annabelle opened the car door and slid into the seat, she caught herself smiling.

I'm going to have the best summer ever.

17

Later that evening, Annabelle sat cross-legged on the living room floor as she brushed Opie. The television was tuned to her favorite show, but she hadn't really been watching the program. She was too busy telling Opie about her new friend, Haley, and everything she had done at circus school.

Annabelle's attention moved to something on the coffee table. It was the little pink book Aunt Sylvia had given her yesterday.

She reached over the top of Opie and picked up the book. Holding it in her hands, she began to recall everything she had done that day. She thought about how she had discovered some of her talents.

I don't have to be the best, and every word doesn't have to be spelled correctly. It doesn't matter. It's my journal! So, what's stopping me from writing in it?

Annabelle couldn't think of a single reason. "I can do this," she said to Opie with determination in her voice.

She sat Opie on the hardwood floor. She picked up a pencil from the coffee table and took a big breath, letting it out slowly. She opened the book to the first page.

And just let Jack try to correct it, she thought with a giggle.

She began to write . . .

Dear Jurnal . . .

About The Author

Dollie Stiemsma wrote *No Pickles for Annabelle* to help inspire everyone that's ever felt alone and misunderstood. Like so many of her readers, Dollie struggles daily with her own learning disabilities. She knows how it feels to be different and not know why. Dollie wants to remind her readers to always believe in themselves and their abilities and to never stop looking for their own unique talents.   The 103 pets sent to Southwest Colorado soon became 114. One of the dogs was pregnant. She gave birth to 11 puppies two days after arriving in Colorado. Ten of the pets were reunited with their family. Seventeen of the animals died. The remaining 87 were placed in loving homes throughout Southwest Colorado.

The La Plata County Humane Society and The Humane Society of Pagosa Springs made this program possible. Their dedicated staffs and volunteers deserve recognition for their efforts.

Thank you to all involved,

Lucky Henry Walker

About The Publisher

Story Shares is a nonprofit focused on supporting the millions of teens and adults who struggle with reading by creating a new shelf in the library specifically for them. The ever-growing collection features content that is compelling and culturally relevant for teens and adults, yet still readable at a range of lower reading levels.

Story Shares generates content by engaging deeply with writers, bringing together a community to create this new kind of book. With more intriguing and approachable stories to choose from, the teens and adults who have fallen behind are improving their skills and beginning to discover the joy of reading. For more information, visit storyshares.org.

Easy to Read. Hard to Put Down.

www.ingramcontent.com/pod-product-compliance
Lightning Source LLC
Chambersburg PA
CBHW051303170626
46809CB00004B/1755